HOW WOULD YOU FEEL IF YOUR DAD WAS GAY?

by Ann Heron & Meredith Maran
illustrated by Kris Kovick

Alyson Wonderland
an imprint of Alyson Publications, Inc.

Typeset and printed in the United States of America.

This is an Alyson Wonderland book from
Alyson Publications, Inc., 40 Plympton St., Boston, Mass. 02118.
Distributed in England by GMP Publishers, P.O. Box 247, London, N17 9QR, England.

First edition, first printing: June 1991

ISBN 1-55583-188-5

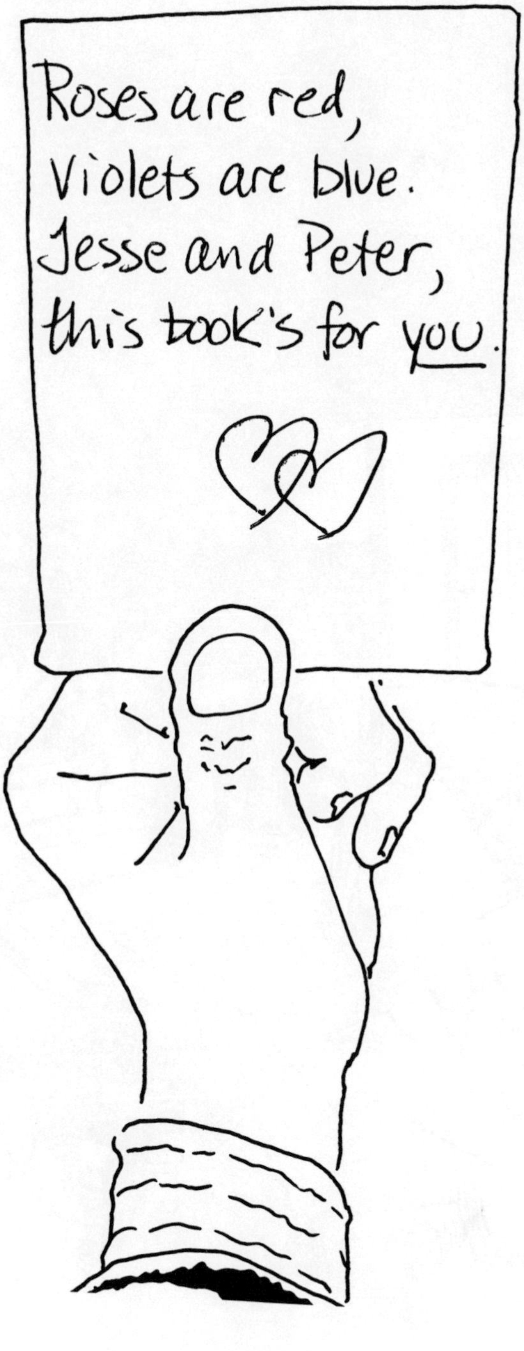
Roses are red,
Violets are blue.
Jesse and Peter,
this book's for you.

It was just after morning recess in Miss Ashford's third grade class. Jasmine and her best friend Maya were whispering to each other when Miss Ashford said, "Settle down, everyone. Father's Day is on Sunday, so we're going to make some cards this morning. But first I thought we could talk a bit about our dads. Who wants to start?"

"My father takes me to baseball games," said Eric.

"My dad tells me great stories every night at bedtime," said Maya.

"I get to go to my dad's for the summer," said David, "and we go swimming practically every day."

"I'm lucky 'cause I have *three* dads," Jasmine said. All the other kids stopped waving their hands at Miss Ashford and stared at Jasmine. Miss Ashford stared at Jasmine, too. Jasmine felt nervous now, but she had to explain.

"My real dad's gay," she said. "My brother and I live with him and his lover, Andrew, half the time. The rest of the time we live with our mama and her new husband. That makes three dads!" To Jasmine it seemed like an hour before anyone stopped staring at her or said a word.

Finally Miss Ashford took her eyes off Jasmine and called on the boy next to her, Sam. "Well *I* have about ten dads," Sam said in a loud voice. "My dad's a fireman and all the guys at the station get me birthday presents and take me to the movies and stuff." Sam looked around to make sure everyone was paying attention to him. But they weren't. All the kids were still looking at Jasmine.

From across the room, Jasmine heard Robert say, "Jasmine's dad is a faggot." Jasmine looked at Maya, but Maya looked away. "Ooh — it's so gross, two men kissing each other," Jennifer said.

And then Paul said, "I'm glad *my* father isn't a sissy."

Jasmine decided to act braver than she felt. "Wait a minute, you guys," she said loudly. "How would you feel if *your* dad was gay?"

"All right, class," said Miss Ashford in an unusually strict voice. "Let's get started on those cards."

Jasmine made three Father's Day cards — one for each of her dads. She worked extra hard to make them just right. But when she was through she didn't feel like showing them to anyone — not even to Maya.

Jasmine ate lunch by herself in her classroom that day because she felt like being alone. When she finished eating she wandered out to the schoolyard. She heard some yelling. Her older brother, Michael, was surrounded by some fifth-grade boys from his class. Michael looked mad, and he was clenching his fists.

"My father is *not* a faggot!" Jasmine heard Michael yell.

The boys started chanting, "Faggot, faggot."

Michael's face was getting madder and madder, and the crowd around Michael was getting bigger. One boy said, "Your dad's a gay punk and so are you." Jasmine had a terrible feeling in her stomach now, and she hoped Michael wouldn't punch anyone.

Jasmine couldn't decide if she should stick up for Michael or stay away from the fight. Then she heard Noah, a boy in Michael's class, say to the others in a quiet voice, "I don't see why it's so bad if Michael's dad is gay. That's his private business."

No one said anything at first. Then one of the boys said, "Hey! Maybe Noah's a faggot too."

Noah looked like he was trying not to cry, and Michael looked like he didn't know *what* to do.

The bell rang, and everyone went back to class. Jasmine worried all afternoon. When she met Michael to walk home together, he didn't say a word. He walked a few steps ahead of her all the way, kicking pebbles angrily.

When they were almost home, Michael said, "What's your *problem*, Jasmine? Why'd you have to open your big mouth about Dad? Do you really want us to spend the rest of our lives getting teased to death?" Jasmine didn't know what to say. Her throat felt like she'd swallowed a pine cone.

By dinnertime Michael hadn't said another word to Jasmine. "Pass the potatoes, Michael," Andrew said. "And could you put a smile on them, please?" Michael frowned and passed the potatoes.

"What's new, Junior Girl?" Ron asked Jasmine. Jasmine glanced at her father and shrugged, then looked down at her plate.

When dinner was over, Ron said, "Okay, you two. What's going on?" Michael glared at Jasmine. "Michael? Feel like talking about it?" Ron asked again.

"What's to talk about?" Michael snapped. "My stupid sister decided to tell the whole school that you guys are gay. She just ruined my life, that's all."

Ron and Andrew looked at each other. Then Andrew pulled Jasmine into his lap, and Ron put his hand on Michael's shoulder. "I'd like to hear both your stories," Ron said.

"I want to talk about my family like other kids do," Jasmine said. "I'm tired of hearing kids say 'faggot' and 'punk' and stuff. They don't even know they're talking about my dad, but it still hurts my feelings."

"Oh, great!" Michael said sarcastically, shaking Ron's hand off his shoulder. "You want *your* friends to know Dad's gay — fine. But I don't want *anyone* to know. If you had to blab you should've waited till I went to junior high.

"Anyway," Michael went on, "when kids call each other 'faggot' they don't even know what the word means. Why can't you just ignore it? That's what I do."

Andrew moved his chair closer to Michael's. "The way I see it, you're both right," he said. "Jas, you have the right to tell the truth about your family, and I sure do understand why you'd want to." Jasmine felt tears in her eyes — the tears she'd been holding in all day. Ron gave her a little squeeze.

"And Mike, you have the right to privacy," Andrew continued. "Maybe someday nobody will care if a person is gay or straight. But that's not true now, and I know how other people's prejudice can hurt. I understand why you'd want to protect yourself from it. If you don't want the kids at school to know your dad and I are

11

gay, you should be able to keep that to yourself. It's not your job to stop them when they use bad words about gay people, either. You have to deal with this however it's best for you."

Michael thought about all the times he'd heard kids call someone "faggot." He'd never said anything, because he was afraid they'd guess his dad was gay. In fact, Michael had even used the word himself a few times, to keep them from guessing. Even though Ron was saying Michael hadn't done anything wrong, Michael felt bad. And he wondered if maybe his little sister was braver than he was.

Andrew and Ron looked at each other again. Andrew added, "Your dad and I feel differently about privacy, too. Your dad tells practically everybody that he's gay. I hardly tell anyone. Partly that's because Ron is his own boss, and my boss might fire me if he found out. Partly it's because your dad and I have different personalities.

"Sometimes," Andrew said, "I wish your dad wouldn't be so open about being gay. And sometimes your dad wishes I would be *more* open. It's not always easy, but we try hard to respect each other's way of handling our differences. That's what you two have to work out, too."

Jasmine's tears spilled out of her eyes and onto the kitchen table. "How *can* we work it out?" Michael asked angrily. "If she had it her way, everyone in the school would know — if they don't already. How can I get any privacy?"

"Jas, maybe you could tell the people you want to tell," Ron said, "but let them know it's personal so they won't tell everyone else. Would that be okay?"

Jasmine sniffled. "Not really. No one else has to keep secrets about their family." Jasmine sneaked a glance at Michael. Now he looked more sad than mad. "But I guess I could try it — for Michael," she said.

"Would it help if there was a grownup at school you could talk to about it?" Ron asked Jasmine.

"Like who?" Jasmine said. "Miss Ashford didn't even stop the kids when they were saying terrible things about gay people. She looked like she agreed with them."

Ron frowned. "You know," he said, "I'm sorry that you've been dealing with this by yourself. I wish I had talked to someone at your school before the school year even started. Maybe it's not too late for me to have a little talk with the principal."

"Oh boy!" said Michael angrily. "That's all I need!"

"Don't worry, son," Ron said. "I'll make sure Mr. Kay knows not to do anything that embarrasses you. I'll just ask him to talk to the teachers so they won't let what happened to both of you today happen again."

"You just don't understand kids," Michael snapped. "There's no way that's gonna work." But secretly, he hoped it would.

Meanwhile, Noah and his mother, Sarah, were having a strange dinner, too. Noah kept trying to talk to Sarah, but Sarah kept jumping up to answer the phone. "Sorry, sweetie," she said when she came back to the table.

"I guess you care more about your *friends* than your *son*," Noah said harshly. Sarah looked surprised and hurt. Noah was kind of surprised, too. He didn't usually talk to his mom that way.

13

"Nothing matters more to me than my son," Sarah said firmly. "And I put the answering machine on so we won't be interrupted again. What's bugging you, anyway?"

Noah shook his head and pushed the food around on his plate. "I just wish you wouldn't talk on the phone so much," he muttered.

Sarah asked, "Yes ... and what else?"

"And I wish ... I wish you weren't a lesbian!" Noah said, and he started to cry.

Sarah put her arms around Noah and said, "Did something happen at school today?"

Noah nodded and blew his nose in a napkin. "This kid Michael got surrounded in the schoolyard," Noah explained. "The kids were calling him 'sissy' and 'punk' and stuff. I guess Michael's sister told her class that their father's gay." Noah started crying again. "I tried to stick up for Michael — then they started calling *me* a faggot."

"Oh, honey," Sarah said. She looked like she wanted to cry, too. "I'm so sorry that happened to you."

"It didn't really happen to me," Noah said. "It mostly happened to Michael. But I had to stick up for him, since we're gay too."

Sarah shook her head. "No, Noah," she said. "*We're* not gay. *I'm* gay. You're eleven years old. You have a long time to figure out who you are and who you love. You may be gay, or you may well be straight. But listen — this is important: It's not up to you to defend gay people, or gay people's kids, just because *I'm* a lesbian. Do you understand that?"

"I guess," Noah said. But he didn't. He went to his room and shut the door.

16

Noah wouldn't let Sarah come into his room until bedtime. "Want some scratchers?" she asked him in a soft voice.

Noah nodded and Sarah started scratching his back, just like she'd done every night for as long as he could remember. "I'm sorry this is so hard on you, Noah," she said. "If it was up to me, nobody would give anybody a hard time about who they love."

"Why do they?" Noah asked her. "Why do so many people think it's bad to be gay?"

"That's a good question," Sarah said quietly. "I really can't answer it. I think people are afraid of anything that seems different. A lot of straight people don't know that gay people feel the same things they do about love and sex and having children, or not having them. They don't know that loving someone of the same sex is just another way of loving."

While Sarah was talking, Noah was thinking about Samantha, a girl in his class he liked. Even though Noah's own mom was gay, he couldn't imagine liking a boy the way he liked Samantha. But he didn't see anything wrong with it if he did, either.

Sarah was quiet for a minute. Then she said, "What matters to me most, Noah, is that you know you can talk to me about this. I know it upsets you to hear bad things about gay people, and I don't want you to have to hold that inside you."

"Okay," Noah said. His eyes felt like they had sand in them. He just wanted to go to sleep.

"Goodnight, sweetie," Sarah said, and she turned out the light.

The next morning Sarah made waffles, Noah's favorite breakfast. When she wasn't looking, Noah peeked in his lunch bag to see if she'd left him one of the little notes she sometimes wrote him. She had. The notes always started "Roses are red, violets are blue...," and they ended with a funny rhyme. Today's poem ended, "and I don't know another eleven-year-old as brave and sweet as you."

Noah thought the poem was kind of mushy, but knowing his mom loved him helped him feel better about going back to school today.

When Michael woke up that morning, the first thing he saw was Andrew picking up Michael's dirty clothes from where Michael had dropped them the night before. "Hi," he said to Andrew. Andrew came over and sat on Michael's bed.

"Hi, yourself, little man," Andrew said with a smile. Michael remembered the things he'd said yesterday.

"You know, it's not all bad that Dad's gay," Michael told Andrew. "If Dad wasn't gay we wouldn't know you."

Andrew's smile got bigger and happier-looking. "I'm glad I know you, too, Michael," Andrew said.

Ron took Michael and Jasmine to school that day, so he could talk to Mr. Kay after school started. Michael was saying good-bye to Ron when he noticed Noah standing nearby. "That's the kid who tried to stick up for me," Michael whispered to Ron. As Ron walked toward the principal's office, Michael and Noah nodded to each other, but they didn't speak.

Jasmine was wondering if Miss Ashford would mention what had happened in class the day before. Actually, she was hoping that Miss Ashford would tell Robert and the other kids to apologize for the mean things they'd said. But Miss Ashford acted like nothing had happened, even when she handed out the Father's Day cards for the kids to take home.

While Jasmine was carefully putting her three cards in her backpack, Maya came up beside her. "I like your cards, Jas," Maya said. "I bet your dads will like them, too."

All of a sudden Jasmine felt really happy. "I hope so," she said, smiling at her best friend.

Michael was worried that the boys who'd called him names in the yard yesterday would do it again today. But they stayed away from him, and Michael stayed away from them.

Just before the bell rang at the end of the day, a shy boy named Joe came up to Michael. "I heard what those jerks were saying yesterday," Joe said in a low voice. "My mom got married to another guy, so I have a dad and a stepfather, too. Big deal if you have three dads."

Michael felt embarrassed, so he looked away. But when the bell rang, Michael dug a pack of gum out of his pocket and offered a piece to Joe.

Noah had been trying to decide all day if he should tell Michael that *he* had a gay parent, too. Noah didn't mind Michael knowing, if Michael would promise not to tell anyone else. But Michael hung out by himself at lunch and recess, acting as if he wanted to be alone.

Right before school ended, Noah got up the nerve to talk to Michael. But just when he started walking over to him, the bell rang and Michael left. Noah was disappointed and relieved at the same time.

When Jasmine and Michael got home from school that day, Ron told them their mother was coming for dinner. "So we can all talk about my conversation with Mr. Kay," Ron said.

Jasmine and Michael were nervous, but Ron smiled and added, "Everything went fine. Mr. Kay seems to understand that letting kids put other kids down because their folks are gay is just as bad as letting kids get put down 'cause they're black. And he promised he'd hold an assembly to talk about families — all kinds of families." Jasmine hoped that meant Miss Ashford would be on her side if kids started picking on her again.

During the next couple of weeks, Jasmine, Michael, and Noah noticed a few little changes at school. One time a kid called another kid "faggot," and Noah and Michael were surprised to hear their teacher tell him not to use that word. Miss Ashford asked Jasmine if her dads liked their Father's Day cards. And Mr. Kay was being extra nice to Jasmine and Michael.

Then one morning the teachers told the kids to line up for a special assembly about families. When Michael stood up he felt dizzy, like the time he had the stomach flu. Jasmine hoped none of the teachers knew the whole school was having a special assembly just because of what she'd said about her three dads.

When the kids and the teachers were sitting in the auditorium, Mr. Kay stepped onto the stage and raised his hand, the signal that meant that everyone should be quiet. All the kids and teachers raised their hands too, until it was almost completely silent in the big room.

"Today we have a special visitor," Mr. Kay said. A woman stepped up beside him. "This is Doctor Larkin," Mr. Kay said. "She's a children's counselor, and she's here to talk to us about some of the different kinds of families there are in the world — and in our school."

"Hi, kids," Doctor Larkin said. Jasmine thought she looked too young to be a doctor. "Before we do any talking, I want to show some slides. Will someone turn out the lights, please?"

A bunch of kids ran for the light switch, the way they always did when someone asked for the lights to be turned off. As soon as the noise stopped, a picture appeared on the screen. It showed two adults and two kids in front of a house. "This is one kind of family," Doctor Larkin said. "A mother, a father, and their two children. How many of you think this is the most normal kind of family there is?"

Almost all the kids raised their hands, including Noah, Michael, and Jasmine.

"Most of these families come about when a man and a woman marry each other and decide to have children," continued Dr. Larkin. "Sometimes they create children together, and sometimes they decide to adopt children who are already born."

The next picture was of a woman and a girl sitting at a kitchen table. "Here's a mother-and-child family. And guess what? I happen to know that almost half of the children in this school live in *this* kind of family — with one parent and one or more children. Does that make this kind of family seem more normal?" A few kids nodded, but most of them didn't say anything.

Now there were two pictures on the screen at once. One showed a boy with a man and a woman. The other showed the same boy with another woman, another man, and three other kids. "When parents get divorced and remarried," Dr. Larkin said, "sometimes kids get a whole new family. Tell me what you think: How many mothers does this boy have?"

"Two!" a few kids called out. "Just one," shouted a girl sitting near Jasmine. Doctor Larkin looked at the girl. "No matter what happens, you still just have one mom," the girl said.

Doctor Larkin nodded and smiled. "It's true that only one woman can give birth to each child," she answered. "But I'm sure lots of you have step-mothers or aunts or family friends who love you as if you were their own. Does anyone know what I mean?" This time lots of kids said, "Yeah," and, "Uh-huh."

The next picture showed a lot of adults and kids gathered in front of a little house that looked like an igloo made of mud. "For lots of people in the world," Doctor Larkin said, "'Family' means everyone you're related to — and the whole family lives together, sometimes in one room." That sounded pretty crowded, but when Jasmine looked at the picture, all the people in it looked happy.

Now there were two pictures on the screen again. One showed two women holding a baby. The other showed two men with a teenaged boy. "These women are gay, and with their baby they make a family. The men are gay too, and they're raising a son together. Do you all know what 'gay' means?" There were giggles and snorts from all over the room. Michael felt like there was a spotlight shining right on his face. Noah slumped down in his chair. Jasmine wished she'd stayed home today.

"A gay woman — a lesbian — is someone who falls in love with a woman. A gay man is someone who falls in love with a man." The giggling and muttering was getting louder.

"It seems that talking about gay people makes some of you nervous," Dr. Larkin said. "That doesn't surprise me. Talking about gay people makes a lot of grownups nervous, too. And their nervousness keeps them from asking questions or learning more about it. That's one reason a lot of people don't understand that being gay is just another way for people to fall in love, and make a family. Lots of gay people have kids. Some have biological children, and some have adopted children, just like other families."

The next picture showed a little boy with three women. One of the women was very old, bent over with lots of wrinkles. One had gray hair but she didn't look too old. The other one looked like a regular mother.

"This is a little boy who lives with his mother, his grandmother, and his great-grandmother!" Doctor Larkin said. "How many of you have great-grandmothers who are still alive?" Only two kids raised their hands. "So this is a *really* unusual family," Doctor Larkin said. "But it's still a family, isn't it?"

Doctor Larkin turned on the lights. Mr. Kay joined her on the stage. "In this school we teach you to respect each other," Mr. Kay said. "No matter what country your ancestors were born in, or what your parents do for a living, or what kind of family you have. Haven't we talked about that before?" A lot of kids said, "Yes."

"If you have questions about what it means to be gay," Mr. Kay went on, "Doctor Larkin is here to answer them. But I want you all to be clear about one thing: It is *not* acceptable for any child in this school to call *anyone* names or treat *anyone* with disrespect. Understood?"

Jasmine just knew no one would have the nerve to ask Doctor Larkin any questions about gay people, and she was right. After a few minutes, Mr. Kay dismissed the assembly.

As she was leaving the auditorium, Jasmine noticed that Michael had his baseball cap pulled way down over his ears, the way he wore it when he was in a bad mood. Jasmine wished she'd never told everyone about her three dads. But then Miss Ashford came up and gave Jasmine a little hug. "I thought that was a very interesting assembly. I guess we all have a lot to learn about families," Miss Ashford said. Suddenly Jasmine felt a lot better.

Noah told his mom about the assembly as soon as she got home from work. "This doctor came and showed slides of different kinds of families — even two lesbians and their baby. It was kind of embarrassing, but it was kind of cool, too. And Mr. Kay told the kids they're not allowed to call anyone bad names like 'faggot' any more."

Sarah looked happy. "That's great, Noah," she said. "Maybe this'll keep you from getting your feelings hurt so often at school. It's a start, anyway." She squeezed Noah's shoulder. "You know, sweetie, I'll understand if you *never* tell anyone I'm a lesbian. You just do what you have to do, okay? And I'll always love you, no matter what." Noah felt kind of embarrassed. But he felt kind of cool, too.

At dinner that night Jasmine kept hoping Michael would mention the assembly, but he didn't. Finally she said, "Daddy, we had our families assembly today. They talked about gay people."

Ron stopped eating and asked, "Feel like telling me about it? Michael?"

Michael shrugged his shoulders. "This lady showed a bunch of slides. It was kinda dumb," he said around a mouthful of food.

"Jas?" Andrew asked. "What did you think?"

Jasmine thought about it for a minute. "It *was* kinda dumb," she said, sneaking a peek at Michael. "But I liked it anyway. I think it helped Miss Ashford understand about our family."

"That's good," Ron said. "I hope it makes Miss Ashford more sensitive to you, Jas. But you know what? What really matters is what *you guys* think and how *you* feel.

"I live my way," Ron went on. "Your mom lives her way. Mr. Kay lives his way. You two are young now, but pretty soon you'll be figuring out how *you* want to live." Andrew nodded and put his hand on Michael's back. "And when you do, don't ever let anybody tell you it's wrong. As long as you're not hurting anyone else, as long as you feel it's right for you, you do it. You hear me?"

Jasmine felt a bit scared by how serious her dad sounded. She went over and plopped into his lap, and he hugged her.

"You know, I'm real proud of both of you," Ron said in a softer voice. "Each of you is finding your own way. Sometimes that means

listening to yourself more than you listen to other people — even your friends or your parents." Ron smiled at Michael and Jasmine, then he and Andrew gave each other a look.

"Good thing we've got a couple of brave, smart kids," Ron said.

Andrew nodded again and put his arm around Michael. "You've got that right," Andrew said.

Later that night Jasmine and Michael were in the bathroom brushing their teeth. Jasmine kept looking at Michael's face to see if he was still in a bad mood. It was hard to tell while his mouth was full of toothpaste. "Michael," she said quietly. He looked at her in the mirror. "I'm sorry I told everyone about Dad and Andrew. I didn't mean to. It just slipped out."

Michael spit out the toothpaste and took a drink of water. Then he gave Jasmine a little punch on the shoulder. "That's okay, Jas," he said in a way that told Jasmine he meant it. "I used to do stuff like that when I was eight, too."

"Anyway," Michael said as he left the bathroom, "if you hadn't said what you said, we wouldn't have had the assembly. If we hadn't had the assembly, Mr. Kay wouldn't've made that rule about not calling kids 'faggot.' I'm glad he made the rule. So I guess in a way I'm glad you said what you did."

31

When Ron and Andrew came in to kiss Jasmine goodnight, she smiled at her dads. "You know how it feels when your dad is gay?" she asked them. "Sometimes it feels kinda weird. But mostly it feels just fine."